HAPPY HAUNTING, AMELIA BEDELIA

By HERMAN PARISH
PICTURES BY LYNN SWEAT

SCHOLASTIC INC.
New York Toronto London Auckland Sydney
Mexico City New Delhi Hong Kong Buenos Aires

ISBN 0-439-66970-7

Published by Scholastic Inc., 557 Broadway, New York, NY 10012,
by arrangement with Greenwillow Books, an imprint of HarperCollins Publishers.
SCHOLASTIC and associated logos are trademarks
and/or registered trademarks of Scholastic Inc.

12 11 10 9 8 7 6 5 4 3 2   5 6 7 8 9 10/0

Printed in the U.S.A.   23

First Scholastic paperback printing, September 2005

Watercolors and a black pen were used to prepare the full-color art.

The text type is Times.

For Margaret,
who hates 'cary masks
—H. P.

To Kevin, Sara, and Ian
—L. S.

When Amelia Bedelia arrived for work,

she could not believe her eyes.

"Oh my gosh," said Amelia Bedelia.

"What has happened to the house?"

6

"This is terrible," said Amelia Bedelia.

"Mr. and Mrs. Rogers must need me.

Someone has ruined their house."

She ran to the front door.

"Aghhh!" yelled Amelia Bedelia. "Help!"

Mr. and Mrs. Rogers rushed outside.

"Hold still," said Mrs. Rogers.

"I will get the bats out of your belfry."

"Ha!" said Mr. Rogers.

"That would be a full-time job.

She has made me bats for years."

"You are untangled, Amelia Bedelia,"

said Mrs. Rogers.

"Come inside and relax."

"Wow," said Amelia Bedelia.

"Who wrecked your house?"

"We did," said Mrs. Rogers.

"We are getting ready for Halloween."

"Is that tonight?" said Amelia Bedelia.

"How did you forget?" said Mr. Rogers.

"Those bats on the front porch

must have made you batty."

"Sorry," said Amelia Bedelia.

"I have been very busy.

I was at school helping children

make their costumes."

"Good for you," said Mrs. Rogers.

"We invited all of our neighbors

for a Halloween party. And you, too.

Tonight, the best costume wins a prize."

"Gosh," said Amelia Bedelia.

"Your house looks so spooky."

"Thank you," said Mrs. Rogers.

"The spookier the better."

"That is the idea," said Mr. Rogers.

"What fun," said Amelia Bedelia.

"I will help you clean up."

"No you don't," said Mr. Rogers.

"I worked hard

to get this place to look shabby."

"Then I will help you mess up,"

said Amelia Bedelia.

"What should I do first?"

"Hand me that hammer,"

said Mr. Rogers.

"But first, crack a window.

It has gotten very warm in here."

KEE-RASH

"Uh-oh," said Amelia Bedelia.

"I tried to just crack it,

but it broke instead."

"Amelia Bedelia!" said Mr. Rogers.

"I meant, open the window a bit."

"It is open," said Amelia Bedelia.

"There are lots of bits . . . and pieces."

"It's not your fault, dear,"

said Mrs. Rogers.

"Besides, that broken window

makes our house

look truly haunted."

Mr. Rogers shook his head and said,

"I think you both have gone batty."

"What is next?" asked Amelia Bedelia.

"Let's see," said Mrs. Rogers.

"A lot of people are coming tonight.

We should add a leaf to the table."

"A leaf?" said Amelia Bedelia.

"Yes, of course," said Mrs. Rogers.

"A leaf or two makes the table larger.

Do you know

where to find the leaves?"

"Of course I do," said Amelia Bedelia.

"Before you go," said Mr. Rogers,

"please hand me that witch."

"That which what?"

said Amelia Bedelia.

"Not what," said Mr. Rogers. "Witch."

"Which what?" said Amelia Bedelia.

"Not which what," said Mr. Rogers.

"That witch there,

with the pointy hat."

Amelia Bedelia held up two witches.

"They both have pointy hats," she said.

"Which witch do you want?"

"Whichever," said Mr. Rogers.

"No, I mean, whatever witch,

which . . . oh, skip it!

Just get those leaves."

Amelia Bedelia skipped away.

"Good thing it is fall,"

said Amelia Bedelia.

"I can get lots of leaves for the table."

She saw something wriggle

under a leaf.

"Sorry, Mister Worm, but back you go,"

she said.

"Yoo-hoo," called Mrs. Rogers

from the kitchen window.

"There is no time to do yard work.

I need your help."

Amelia Bedelia went inside.

"There we go," said Amelia Bedelia.

"Now the table looks smaller to me,

but it is so much prettier.

Mrs. Rogers always has great ideas."

Amelia Bedelia went into the kitchen.

"There you are," said Mrs. Rogers.

"You are so creative with food.

Let's cook up some gruesome goodies."

"Goody," said Amelia Bedelia.

THIS WORM CASSEROLE NEEDS MORE SPAGHETTI.

MMMMM! CRANBERRY JUICE MAKES A TASTY VAMPIRE PUNCH.

CRUMBLE UP COOKIES FOR THE KITTY LITTER CAKE.

WE NEED MORE EYEBALLS.

I'LL PEEL ANOTHER BUNCH OF GRAPES.

DRIED APRICOTS MAKE DELICIOUS EARS.

There was a knock at the kitchen door.

"Trick or treat," said Cousin Alcolu.

"I do not know any tricks,"

said Amelia Bedelia.

"But you can sample some treats."

"Thank you," said Cousin Alcolu.

Mr. Rogers walked into the kitchen.

"Something smells good," he said.

"Well, it sure isn't me,"

said Cousin Alcolu.

"I have been working very hard.

I harvested a load of pumpkins

for the party tonight."

"How generous," said Mr. Rogers.

"Do you know how to carve

jack-o'-lanterns?"

"I did one," said Cousin Alcolu.

He showed them his pumpkin.

"That face looks very familiar,"

said Amelia Bedelia.

Mrs. Rogers tried not to laugh.

"Very funny," said Mr. Rogers.

"But that pumpkin is too handsome.

Have you got anything scarier?"

"Wait here," said Cousin Alcolu.

He went out to his truck.

Cousin Alcolu returned

with the scariest scarecrow ever.

"Meet Oswald," said Cousin Alcolu.

"He scares away birds for miles."

"Ooooooh!" said Mrs. Rogers.

"He sends shivers down my spine.

Oswald can sit here for tonight."

"He doesn't scare me," said Mr. Rogers.

"I do not know the meaning

of the word fear."

"You don't?" said Amelia Bedelia.

"The word 'fear' is in the dictionary.

I will look it up for you."

"Show me later," said Mr. Rogers.

"I must get my costume ready.

I am going to be

a circus strongman."

"And I am going to be a queen,"

said Mrs. Rogers.

"Amelia Bedelia, what is

your costume going to be?"

31

"Gee," said Amelia Bedelia.

"I do not have a costume."

"Sure you do," said Mr. Rogers.

"You wear a costume every day."

Mrs. Rogers glared at her husband.

"What do you mean?"

said Amelia Bedelia.

"These are my clothes, not a costume.

I have always dressed like this."

Mr. Rogers felt bad about

what he had said.

He was too embarrassed

to say anything.

"Come along, Amelia Bedelia,"

said Mrs. Rogers.

"I have an idea for you . . .

and for Cousin Alcolu."

"See you tonight?" said Mr. Rogers.

Amelia Bedelia did not reply.

That night, as darkness fell,

the house really did look haunted.

Spooky music with scary sounds

made it even more fun.

Floorboards creaked.

Chains rattled.

Moans and groans

filled the air.

CLANTY-
CLANK-
KLUNK

AI-YEEEEEE

The doorbell rang.

"Our first trick-or-treaters,"

said Mrs. Rogers.

"Would you get the front door, dear?"

"Yes, Your Majesty," said Mr. Rogers.

As soon as he was out of sight,

Mrs. Rogers ran to the back door.

While Mr. Rogers
handed out treats
at the front door . . .

Mrs. Rogers
let in a trick
at the back door.

"Right this way," said Mr. Rogers.

"Thank you," said a skeleton.

"I was dying to come in."

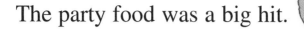

The party food was a big hit.

"Care for an eyeball?"

said a girl to her dad.

"Yuck!" he said.

"Yum," she said.

"They are good and disgusting."

"Try some finger food,"

said Mr. Rogers.

"Oh, cool!" said the boy.

"These cookies have little fingers."

"They were Amelia Bedelia's idea,"

said Mr. Rogers.

"Where is she?" asked the boy.

"Good question," said Mr. Rogers.

"May I have two cups of blood?"

asked a girl.

"My pleasure," said Mrs. Rogers.

"I love your costumes."

"Amelia Bedelia helped us,"

said a little boy.

"Wonderful," said Mrs. Rogers.

"Maybe you will win the prize."

"Have you seen Amelia Bedelia?"

asked Mr. Rogers.

"Not yet," said Mrs. Rogers.

"She might not come,

thanks to you."

"What did I do wrong?"

said Mr. Rogers.

"You know," said Mrs. Rogers.

"You made fun of her clothes."

"I feel terrible," said Mr. Rogers.

"I will apologize when I see her."

Just then Mr. Rogers shuddered.

"What is wrong?" said Mrs. Rogers.

"It sounds silly," said Mr. Rogers.

"That scarecrow gives me the creeps."

"Scaredy-cat," said Mrs. Rogers.

"It looks alive," said Mr. Rogers.

"I feel like it is watching me."

Ding-dong!

Mr. Rogers jumped.

"Relax," said Mrs. Rogers.

"You are imagining things.

Go and see who is at the door."

Mr. Rogers opened the door.

He smiled a big smile.

"Well, well," he said.

"I have never been so glad

to see a ghost. Do come in,

Amelia . . . uh, Miss Ghost."

"WOOOOOOOO!" said the ghost

as it floated into the house.

Mr. Rogers was a perfect host.

"Care for refreshments?"

he asked.

The ghost shook its head no.

"Well," said Mr. Rogers,

"would you like to judge

our costume contest?"

The ghost nodded yes.

"Attention, everyone," said Mrs. Rogers.

"It is time for our Halloween contest.

Anyone who wishes to compete

for the prize, step right this way."

"I am Sonny Day,

your T.V. weatherman.

I forecast that I will win!"

"You can't beat peace and love.

This hippie has the grooviest

'tea' shirt and 'bell' bottoms."

"If I win,

I will still

be in a pickle!"

"I am all eyes."

"I am all ears."

"And I am

right under your nose."

"Bravo!" said Mrs. Rogers.

"Yes," said Mr. Rogers.

"I can tell that Amelia Bedelia

helped them a lot. Too bad

she could not be here tonight."

He winked at Mrs. Rogers.

Just then the clock struck ten.

"Okay, everyone," said Mrs. Rogers.

"Time to take off your masks."

"Uh-oh!" said the ghost.

It tried to slip away.

"Whoa there," said Mr. Rogers.

"It's time I put my foot down."

Mr. Rogers stepped on the sheet.

As the ghost kept walking,

the sheet was pulled off to reveal . . .

"Cousin Alcolu!" said Mr. Rogers.

"Where is Amelia Bedelia?"

Cousin Alcolu looked very afraid.

He pointed behind Mr. Rogers.

He opened his mouth to speak,

but he was scared speechless.

Mr. Rogers wheeled around.

"BOO!" screamed the scarecrow.

"Yiiiiii!" yelled Mr. Rogers.

He threw his barbell up in the air.

Mr. Rogers turned around

and ran right into Cousin Alcolu.

They both fell in a heap.

"Happy Halloween!"

said Amelia Bedelia.

"Amelia Bedelia!"

said Mr. Rogers.

"Ha-ha," said Cousin Alcolu.

"I think you should call her

Amelia *Boo*delia."

"As your queen," said Mrs. Rogers,

"I declare Amelia Bedelia the winner

for the best costume."

The next day Amelia Bedelia

and Cousin Alcolu

came to help clean up.

"Great party," said Cousin Alcolu.

"Thank you," said Mrs. Rogers.

"We will do it again next year.

Start planning your costume now."

"I will," said Amelia Bedelia.

"But you have the best ideas."

"Those trick-or-treaters!" said Mr. Rogers.

"Somebody piled leaves on our table."

"That was me," said Amelia Bedelia.

"That was lovely," said Mrs. Rogers.

"They made a beautiful centerpiece."

Mrs. Rogers showed Amelia Bedelia

how to add a leaf to the table.

"There we go," said Mrs. Rogers.

"Now let's set the table for lunch."

"Amelia Bedelia," said Mr. Rogers.

"I apologize for what I said yesterday."

"Apology accepted,"

said Amelia Bedelia.

"Try some leftover

Worm Casserole."

Mr. Rogers took a huge portion.

"It is very tasty," he said.

"Glad you like it," said Amelia Bedelia.

"I got worried yesterday

when I ran out of spaghetti."

"You ran out?" asked Mr. Rogers.

He took a closer look at his food.

"Then what is this?" said Mr. Rogers.

"Lucky me," said Amelia Bedelia.

"Every leaf I picked up in your yard

had a fat, juicy worm under it."

Mr. Rogers turned as green as a witch.

"Trick or treat!" said Amelia Bedelia,

laughing.